3800 17 0056029 9
HIGH LIFE HIGHLAND
D0590379
HIGHLAND LIBRARIES
WITHDRAWN

For a united world ...
Britta

CATERPILLAR BOOKS
An imprint of Little Tiger Group
1 The Coda Centre, 189 Munster Road, London SW6 6AW
www.littletiger.co.uk • First published in Great Britain 2017
Text and illustrations copyright © Britta Teckentrup 2017
All rights reserved • ISBN: 978-1-84857-586-8
Printed in China • CPB/1800/0592/0117
10 9 8 7 6 5 4 3 2 1

Under the Same Sky

by Britta Teckentrup

HIGH LIFE HIGHLAND LIBRARIES	
38001700560299	
BERTRAMS	28/04/2017
	£10.99
JF	

We live under
the same sky ...

... in lands
near and far.

... wherever
we are.

... in the cold ice
and snow.

We feel
the same
love ...

... where soft
meadows grow.

We play the
same games ...

... where the hills touch the sky.

... where the grass grows so high.

We sing the same songs ...

... across the same seas.

... caught on the breeze.

...

where
dark
forests
grow.

We
face
the
same
storms
...

...
where
wild
rivers
flow.

... whatever
the weather.

We dream
the same dreams ...

and we dream them ...

... together.

FESTIVAL OF FREEBIES!

WIN A RADIO CASSETTE RECORDER!

MY GUY

16p

No. 33
EVERY SATURDAY
14th OCTOBER 1978

NEW PHOTO STORY!

What sort of guy would she get from–

THE LOVE MACHINE

STAR GUY

CRAZEE ABOUT HIM! (Captain Ken, of course!)

PROBLEM STORY 'My guy's not a real man!'

AUSTRALIA 35c NEW ZEALAND 35c SOUTH AFRICA 35c MALAYSIA $1.25

AMAZING ADAM ANT PIN-UP!

MY GUY

22p

No. 1
EVERY SATURDAY 4th JULY 19

COMPLETE PHOTO STORY

STAND AND DELIVER

Her secret–or her life!

ASTRAL BEAUTY Part 3

Find out fate's face for you!

STAR GUY

THE LUCK OF THE IRISH!

How the Moondogs made it overnight

PHOTO PROBLEM I'm always in tears at parties!

AUSTRALIA 50c NEW ZEALAND 50c MALAYSIA $1.50

NEW! REAL LIFE, REAL LOVE–IN PHOTOS!

MY GUY

14p

EVERY SATURDAY No. 3 18th MARCH 1978

40 PAGES

FREE!

HAPPY HEART BADGE

HOW DEEP IS THEIR LOVE?

IT COULD BE WORTH £100 TO YOU!

BOYS JUST SAY 'NO' TO ME!

See how you could lose out in love...

NEW PHOTO STORY: DON'T PLAY WITH FIRE!

AUSTRALIA 35c NEW ZEALAND 35c SOUTH AFRICA 35c MALAYSIA $1.25

Grease! READ THE ROCK 'N' ROLL LOVE STORY INSIDE

MY GUY

16p

No. 3
EVERY SATURDAY 18th NOVEMBER 197

NEW PHOTO STORY!

When Tessa's around...

GIRLS MUST BE GUYS!

MUST HE GET UPSET?

STAR GUY

TEMPTING TARGET! The hunk you love to hate...

PHOTO PROBLEM SHOULD I BEG FOR HER BOY?

AUSTRALIA 35c NEW ZEALAND 35c SOUTH AFRICA 35c MALAYSIA $1.25